Thanksgiving Day

Nov 28, 1991

[redacted]

Ruminations

[redacted]

[redacted]

[redacted]

WILLIAM STEIG

RUMINATIONS

PREFACE BY WHITNEY BALLIETT

Farrar, Straus and Giroux
NEW YORK

Library of Congress catalog card number: 84-45423
Published simultaneously in Canada by Collins Publishers, Toronto
Printed in the United States of America
Designed by Janet Halverson
First edition, 1984
Many of the drawings in this book originally appeared in *The New Yorker*

On William Steig

William Steig describes himself in *Who's Who* as an "artist," and that seems right. He still behaves like a cartoonist—that is, every Friday he mails several drawings from his home in Connecticut to *The New Yorker,* which buys enough to allow itself the luxury of printing one almost every week. But Steig has long since crossed the mysterious line that separates cartoonists from artists. (This line separates reviewers from critics, versifiers from poets, jazz embellishers from improvisers.) Cartoonists are sketchers who deal in obsolescence; artists, more heavily equipped, aim at permanence. Those few cartoonists, like Steig, who are also artists make you laugh, then lead you to their drawings. There is sleight of hand here. The artist stays out of the way of the joke (you will rarely see a funny cluttered cartoon, unless clutter itself is part of the joke), yet he draws well enough to keep you after the laughter stops.

It took Steig a long time to reach his present vision. His first cartoon appeared in *The New Yorker* on August 9, 1930. (Since the retirement of E. B. White, Steig has become *The New Yorker*'s longest-running contributor. He may even have surpassed White, who began selling to the magazine five years before Steig but has done little during the past fifteen years.) In the cartoon, a convict tells his cell mate: "My youngest is a terror. We can't do a thing with 'im." Two weeks later, the magazine printed his second cartoon. A scrawny Milquetoast in bathing trunks is toweling himself in a locker room and singing, "Oh, Mademoiselle from Armentières," while nearby a group of muscly semi-nude men tell each other of their conquests. Social irony and social paradox, continuing Steig concerns, were immediately clear. His early cartoons are complete drawings. The women are robust, the men big. Their faces are strong and individual. The figures have a Blakean heft, and the drawings are full of detail. They are the work of a recent art-school graduate, which Steig at the time was. Since then, he has slowly transformed his drawings from the traditional to the semi-abstract and the almost surrealistic. This transformation was first visible in the early fifties. His drawings became looser, the figures less substantial. On January 2, 1954, *The New Yorker* ran a Steig drawing of a man at a masquerade party holding his head in his lap. The head has a Picasso face (crookedy, with mismatched eyes), and the lines of the drawing resemble Picasso's later curlicues. Picasso, one of Steig's idols, had appeared. Steig's experimental drawings grew in number and imaginativeness, and by the early sixties he seemed to have completed his revolution. Picasso continues to flicker through his work, and so do Braque and Matisse and even Vuillard. And he likes to pretend he is dabbling in various techniques: a number of drawings in *Ruminations* look exactly like woodcuts. (In a recent exhibition of his work at the Schiller-Wapner Gallery in New York, Steig added color to some of the drawings, and the effect was magical. They became three-dimensional.)

As Steig's drawings have emptied visually, they have filled with meaning—and sometimes mystery. Try "Early risers," which shows three flat figures that appear to have been carved from wood and nailed together either by primitives or by children. The figures' arms are outstretched, and they are in knee-length grass. And try an untitled drawing that shows four motionless human figures, their bodies and heads pressed together, and posed at the edge of a field. Or still another untitled work, done like a woodcut, in which three slightly ominous men in fedoras are standing with a small dog in some sort of vegetation, their arms misshapen and hanging loose. But other drawings of this kind practically embrace you. These include the funny, ingenious "Space exploration," in which an ample, long-haired woman (one of the Pleiades?) is lying on her side in the sky, supporting on her upper side three small astronomers in medieval hoods who are studying space; "Animal, vegetable, mineral," wherein a tall cat, a kind of flower (with a face), and a big rock (with an old man's face) are side by side; and a landscape, called "The pervading melancholy," in which seventeen figures, male and female, are standing or lying down in various attitudes of dismay, puzzlement, and resignation.

Another major group of Steig's present drawings are done almost as portraits. Their subjects stare directly at you, as if they were in nineteenth-century photographs or paintings. Generally the figure is motionless, as in the marvelous "Parfait," in which a beautiful moonfaced woman in a décolleté gown and with a feather in her hair is holding a spoonful of ice cream in her right hand. See also "Bachelor," "A pause in the day's occupation," and "Traveling salesman." Many of these figures—you can almost hear their stillness—are in nineteenth-century garb. Whatever Steig's reasons, another resonant dimension is added. The walls of the twentieth century, which he finds increasingly confining, fall away, and we are in the echoing (and often bucolic) past.

Steig is a handsome, witty, gentle man who doesn't look much different from the way he did twenty years ago. He has a long Van Wyck Brooks brush cut, and small hands. He is neat and composed. He likes to make you laugh, but his own laughter is inturned and oblique. He doesn't much like to talk about himself, but here are some of the things he said on one of his infrequent trips to New York: "I was born on November 14, 1907, in the Bronx. My folks were Joseph and Laura [Ebel], and they came over from Poland early in the century. They were socialists. My father was a housepainter and my mother a seamstress, and eventually both became exhibiting artists. I was next to the last of four boys. Henry was a jazz musician, a cartoonist, a novelist, a photographer, and eventually a designer of jewelry. Irwin was a writer and artist, and Arthur is a poet and artist. After high school, I went to CCNY, where I played water polo and became an all-American. It was the only thing I enjoyed about school. But I was too young to be in college and my father didn't care for my grades. So I switched to the National Academy of Design in 1925, and went for four years. It was then that I sold my first drawings to the old *Life* and to *Judge*. I did cartoons and I did some wood carvings. In fact, I had a show of wood carvings at the Downtown Gallery in 1939. They were influenced by African sculptures somewhat. Nelson Rockefeller bought six of them at one hundred and fifty dollars apiece.

"I started doing children's books in the sixties. I can write one in a week, but it takes me a month to illustrate it. I don't really enjoy illustrating, and my book illustrations are not as good as my *New Yorker* drawings. The reason, probably, is that they are not free. I never jump out of a chair and say: I have a great idea for a story. Generally, I decide it's time to have an idea, and it comes.

"I'm crazy about Picasso, but one is influenced by everything one sees. I used to start a drawing with an idea in mind, but now I draw without knowing what I am going to do. I start with a head and whatever it is that dictates the expression on its face dictates what happens after that. The last thing to come is the title. I work in fits and starts. I'll drive to Kent and get the papers, then do the crossword, and maybe not settle down until close to dinnertime. But I manage to send in five or six drawings a week to *The New Yorker.*

"I have three children. Jeremy is the jazz flutist

and an artist. Maggie is a metalsmith and an improvisational comic. And Lucy is a good painter on her way to being a psychiatrist."

A few more particulars: he has been married four times, and his first wife was Margaret Mead's sister. He has published nearly thirty books, including children's books and collections of drawings. There are one hundred and fifty pictures in *Ruminations*, all of them done during the past six years. A quarter of them are from *The New Yorker.*

Steig's drawings are unique. They are often funny and often moving, and they are always true and shrewd and humane. They please our eye and light our mind. They are continually surprising. If they are improvisations, as Steig says, they come from a lode way inside, an original and beautiful place that he and we have long been at the mercy of.

Whitney Balliett

Ruminations

The captain's vision of his wife

Over the fence

Les baigneuses

Pastoral scene

Chicken fanciers

Appalachian spring

City slicker

Folklorist

Hen party

Flock

A lover and his lass

Recalcitrant horse

Animal, vegetable, mineral

Pet chicken

The writer in his den

"Down!"

Rare moth

Flora and fauna

Minnesinger and maiden

The eternal sea

Gypsy camp

Mulligan stew

Newlyweds

Carousers

In the weeds

Early risers

Clowning for the camera

The pervading melancholy

Tiptoes

Ending of the rain

Unexpected balmy weather

Hyde Park

Genius

Still life with figures

Winter underwear

Kabuki theater

W. Steig

Spring

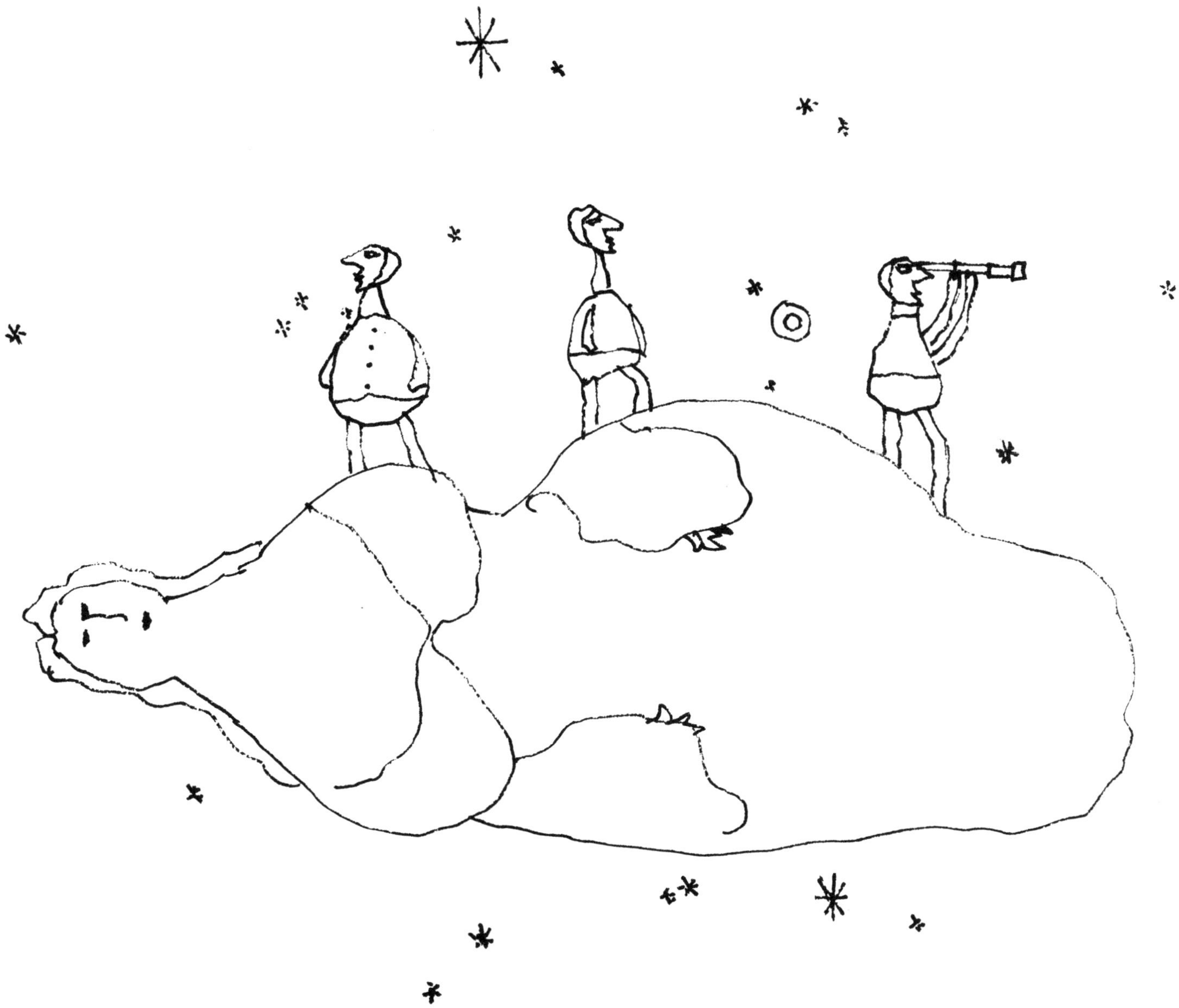

Space exploration

Waiting for the train whistle

Sweethearts since childhood

Up the lazy river

Eloise, Abigail, and Veronica

Traveling salesman

The Sprats

Demesne

Beer garden

At the track

Travelers abroad

Zoological gardens

Public park

Paragon

Strollers

Preliminary survey

At the Rochambeau

Con artists

Musicale

Waiting for silence

Impostors entering a room

Family crisis

On the carpet

Old friends meet again

Kingpin

Spat

Beneficial exercise

"What's the world coming to?"

Floating deity

Cabin fever

The dark

The Claremont Athletic and Social Club

First quarrel

Indian summer

The artist's wife

Meditation

Begone, dull care

W. Steig

A drop too much

Prurient interest

Bachelor

Parfait

Gourmet club

Getting it off the ground

The three Fates

Two sisters look at their new home

A bar in the wrong neighborhood

Wall-to-wall carpeting

Demographic study

Sanctuary

Enchanted isle

Bosky dell

A pause in the day's occupation

A rare day in June

"...But the man who rejoiceth in the Self with the Self is satisfied, and is content in the Self, for him verily there is nothing to do; for him there is no interest in things done in this world, nor any in things not done..."